The River Bank

from The Wind in the Willows

by Kenneth Grahame

illustrated by Adrienne Adams

Methuen Children's Books · London

W1

First published in Great Britain in 1978 by
Methuen Children's Books Limited,
11 New Fetter Lane, London EC4P 4EE.
Illustrations Copyright © 1977 Adrienne Adams

ISBN 0 416 87090 2
Printed in Great Britain
By Sackville Press Billericay Ltd,
Billericay, Essex.

THE Mole had been working very hard all the morning, spring-cleaning his little home. First with brooms, then with dusters; then on ladders and steps and chairs, with a brush and a pail of whitewash; till he had dust in his throat and eyes, and splashes of whitewash all over his black fur, and an aching back and weary arms. Spring was moving in the air above and in the earth below and around him, penetrating even his dark and lowly little house with its spirit of divine discontent and longing. It was small wonder, then, that he suddenly flung down his brush on the floor, said "Bother!" and "O blow!" and also "Hang spring-cleaning!" and bolted out of the house without even waiting to put on his coat. Something up above was calling him imperiously, and he made for the steep little tunnel which answered in his case to the gravelled carriage-drive

owned by animals whose residences are nearer to the sun and air. So he scraped and scratched and scrabbled and scrooged, and then he scrooged again and scrabbled and scratched and scraped, working busily with his little paws and muttering to himself, "Up we go! Up we go!" till at last, pop! his snout came out into the sunlight, and he found himself rolling in the warm grass of a great meadow.

"This is fine!" he said to himself. "This is better than whitewashing!" The sunshine struck hot on his fur, soft breezes caressed his heated brow, and after the seclusion of the cellarage he had lived in so long the carol of happy birds fell on his dulled hearing almost like a shout. Jumping off all his four legs at once, in the joy of living and the delight of spring without its cleaning, he pursued his way across the meadow till he reached the hedge on the further side.

"Hold up!" said an elderly rabbit at the gap. "Sixpence for the privilege of passing by the private road!" He was bowled over in an instant by the impatient and contemptuous Mole, who trotted along the side of the hedge chaffing the other rabbits as they peeped hurriedly from their holes to see what the row was about. "Onion-sauce! Onion-sauce!" he remarked jeeringly, and was gone before they could think of a thoroughly satisfactory reply. Then they all started grumbling at each other. "How *stupid* you are! Why didn't you tell him——" "Well, why didn't *you* say——" "You might have reminded him——" and so on, in the usual way; but, of course, it was then much too late, as is always the case.

It all seemed too good to be true. Hither and thither through the meadows he rambled busily, along the hedge-rows, across the copses, finding everywhere birds building, flowers budding, leaves thrusting—everything happy, and progressive, and occupied. And instead of having an uneasy conscience pricking him and whispering "White-wash!" he somehow could only feel how jolly it was to be the only idle dog among all these busy citizens. After all, the best part of a holiday is perhaps not so much to be rest-ing yourself, as to see all the other fellows busy working.

He thought his happiness was complete when, as he meandered aimlessly along, suddenly he stood by the edge of a full-fed river. Never in his life had he seen a river

before—this sleek, sinuous, full-bodied animal, chasing and chuckling, gripping things with a gurgle and leaving them with a laugh, to fling itself on fresh playmates that shook themselves free, and were caught and held again. All was a-shake and a-shiver—glints and gleams and sparkles, rustle and swirl, chatter and bubble. The Mole was bewitched, entranced, fascinated. By the side of the river he trotted as one trots, when very small, by the side of a man who holds one spellbound by exciting stories; and when tired at last, he sat on the bank, while the river still chattered on to him, a babbling procession of the best stories in the world, sent from the heart of the earth to be told at last to the insatiable sea.

As he sat on the grass and looked across the river, a dark hole in the bank opposite, just above the water's edge, caught his eye, and dreamily he fell to considering what a nice snug dwelling-place it would make for an animal with few wants and fond of a bijou riverside residence, above flood level and remote from noise and dust. As he gazed, something bright and small seemed to twinkle down in the heart of it, vanished, then twinkled once more like a tiny star. But it could hardly be a star in such an unlikely situation; and it was too glittering and small for a glow-worm. Then, as he looked, it winked at him, and so declared itself to be an eye; and a small face began gradually to grow up round it, like a frame round a picture.

A brown little face, with whiskers.

A grave round face, with the same twinkle in its eye that had first attracted his notice.

Small neat ears and thick silky hair.

It was the Water Rat!

Then the two animals stood and regarded each other cautiously.

"Hullo, Mole!" said the Water Rat.

"Hullo, Rat!" said the Mole.

"Would you like to come over?" inquired the Rat presently.

"Oh, it's all very well to *talk*," said the Mole rather pettishly, he being new to a river and riverside life and its ways.

The Rat said nothing, but stooped and unfastened a rope and hauled on it; then lightly stepped into a little boat which the Mole had not observed. It was painted blue outside and white within, and was just the size for two animals; and the Mole's whole heart went out to it at once, even though he did not yet fully understand its uses.

The Rat sculled smartly across and made fast. Then he held up his fore-paw as the Mole stepped gingerly down. "Lean on that!" he said. "Now then, step lively!" and the Mole to his surprise and rapture found himself actually seated in the stern of a real boat.

"This has been a wonderful day!" said he, as the Rat shoved off and took to the sculls again. "Do you know, I've never been in a boat before in all my life."

"What?" cried the Rat, open-mouthed: "Never been in a—you never—well, I—what have you been doing, then?"

"Is it so nice as all that?" asked the Mole shyly, though he was quite prepared to believe it as he leant back in his seat and surveyed the cushions, the oars, the rowlocks, and all the fascinating fittings, and felt the boat sway lightly under him.

"Nice? It's the *only* thing," said the Water Rat solemnly, as he leant forward for his stroke. "Believe me, my young friend, there is *nothing*—absolutely nothing—half so much worth doing as simply messing about in boats. Simply messing," he went on dreamily: "messing—about—in—boats; messing——"

"Look ahead, Rat!" cried the Mole suddenly.

It was too late. The boat struck the bank full tilt. The dreamer, the joyous oarsman, lay on his back at the bottom of the boat, his heels in the air.

"—about in boats—or *with* boats," the Rat went on composedly, picking himself up with a pleasant laugh. "In or out of 'em, it doesn't matter. Nothing seems really to matter, that's the charm of it. Whether you get away, or whether you don't; whether you arrive at your destination or whether you reach somewhere else, or whether you never get anywhere at all, you're always busy, and you never do anything in particular; and when you've done it there's always something else to do, and you can do it if you like, but you'd much better not. Look here! If you've really nothing else on hand this morning, supposing we drop down the river together, and have a long day of it?"

The Mole waggled his toes from sheer happiness,

spread his chest with a sigh of full contentment, and leaned back blissfully into the soft cushions. "*What* a day I'm having!" he said. "Let us start at once!"

"Hold hard a minute, then!" said the Rat. He looped the painter through a ring in his landing-stage, climbed up into his hole above, and after a short interval reappeared staggering under a fat, wicker luncheon-basket.

"Shove that under your feet," he observed to the Mole, as he passed it down into the boat. Then he untied the painter and took the sculls again.

"What's inside it?" asked the Mole, wiggling with curiosity.

"There's cold chicken inside it," replied the Rat briefly; "coldtonguecoldhamcoldbeefpickledgherkinssaladfrench

rollscresssandwidgespottedmeatgingerbeerlemonadesoda
water—"

"O stop, stop," cried the Mole in ecstasies: "This is too
much!"

"Do you really think so?" inquired the Rat seriously.
"It's only what I always take on these little excursions; and
the other animals are always telling me that I'm a mean
beast and cut it *very* fine!"

The Mole never heard a word he was saying. Absorbed
in the new life he was entering upon, intoxicated with the
sparkle, the ripple, the scents and the sounds and the
sunlight, he trailed a paw in the water and dreamed long
waking dreams. The Water Rat, like the good little fellow
he was, sculled steadily on and forbore to disturb him.

"I like your clothes awfully, old chap," he remarked after some half an hour or so had passed. "I'm going to get a black velvet smoking suit myself some day, as soon as I can afford it."

"I beg your pardon," said the Mole, pulling himself together with an effort. "You must think me very rude; but all this is so new to me. So—this—is—a—River!"

"*The* River," corrected the Rat.

"And you really live by the river? What a jolly life!"

"By it and with it and on it and in it," said the Rat. "It's brother and sister to me, and aunts, and company, and food and drink, and (naturally) washing. It's my world, and I don't want any other. What it hasn't got is not worth having, and what it doesn't know is not worth knowing. Lord! the times we've had together! Whether in winter or summer, spring or autumn, it's always got its fun and its excitements. When the floods are on in February, and my cellars and basement are brimming with drink that's no good to me, and the brown water runs by my best bedroom window; or again when it all drops away and shows patches of mud that smells like plum-cake, and the rushes and weed clog the channels, and I can potter about dryshod over most of the bed of it and find fresh food to eat, and things careless people have dropped out of boats!"

"But isn't it a bit dull at times?" the Mole ventured to ask. "Just you and the river, and no one else to pass a word with?"

"No one else to—well, I mustn't be hard on you," said

the Rat with forbearance. "You're new to it, and of course you don't know. The bank is so crowded nowadays that many people are moving away altogether. O no, it isn't what it used to be, at all. Otters, kingfishers, dabchicks, moorhens, all of them about all day long and always wanting you to *do* something—as if a fellow had no business of his own to attend to!"

"What lies over *there?*" asked the Mole, waving a paw towards a background of woodland that darkly framed the water-meadows on one side of the river.

"That? O, that's just the Wild Wood," said the Rat shortly. "We don't go there very much, we river-bankers."

"Aren't they—aren't they very *nice* people in there?" said the Mole a trifle nervously.

"W-e-ll," replied the Rat, "let me see. The squirrels are all right. *And* the rabbits—some of 'em, but rabbits are a mixed lot. And then there's Badger, of course. He lives right in the heart of it; wouldn't live anywhere else, either, if you paid him to do it. Dear old Badger! Nobody interferes with *him*. They'd better not," he added significantly.

"Why, who *should* interfere with him?" asked the Mole.

"Well, of course—there—are others," explained the Rat in a hesitating sort of way. "Weasels—and stoats—and foxes—and so on. They're all right in a way—I'm very good friends with them—pass the time of day when we meet, and all that—but they break out sometimes, there's no denying it, and then—well, you can't really trust them, and that's the fact."

The Mole knew well that it is quite against animal-etiquette to dwell on possible trouble ahead, or even to allude to it; so he dropped the subject.

"And beyond the Wild Wood again?" he asked: "Where it's all blue and dim, and one sees what may be hills or perhaps they mayn't, and something like the smoke of towns, or is it only cloud-drift?"

"Beyond the Wild Wood comes the Wide World," said the Rat. "And that's something that doesn't matter, either to you or me. I've never been there, and I'm never going, nor you either, if you've got any sense at all. Don't ever refer to it again, please. Now then! Here's our backwater at last, where we're going to lunch."

Leaving the main stream, they now passed into what seemed at first sight like a little land-locked lake. Green turf sloped down to either edge, brown snaky tree-roots gleamed below the surface of the quiet water, while ahead of them the silvery shoulder and foamy tumble of a weir, arm-in-arm with a restless dripping mill-wheel, that held up in its turn a grey-gabled mill-house, filled the air with a soothing murmur of sound, dull and smothery, yet with little clear voices speaking up cheerfully out of it at intervals. It was so very beautiful that the Mole could only hold up both fore-paws and gasp, "O my! O my! O my!"

The Rat brought the boat alongside the bank, made her fast, helped the still awkward Mole safely ashore, and swung out the luncheon-basket.

The Mole begged as a favour to be allowed to unpack it

all by himself; and the Rat was very pleased to indulge him, and to sprawl at full length on the grass and rest, while his excited friend shook out the tablecloth and spread it, took out all the mysterious packets one by one and arranged their contents in due order, still gasping, "O my! O my!" at each fresh revelation. When all was ready, the Rat said, "Now, pitch in, old fellow!" and the Mole was

indeed very glad to obey, for he had started his spring-cleaning at a very early hour that morning, as people *will* do, and had not paused for bite or sup; and he had been through a very great deal since that distant time which now seemed so many days ago.

"What are you looking at?" said the Rat presently, when the edge of their hunger was somewhat dulled, and the Mole's eyes were able to wander off the tablecloth a little.

"I am looking," said the Mole, "at a streak of bubbles that I see travelling along the surface of the water. That is a thing that strikes me as funny."

"Bubbles? Oho!" said the Rat, and chirruped cheerily in an inviting sort of way.

A broad glistening muzzle showed itself above the edge
of the bank, and the Otter hauled himself out and shook
the water from his coat.

"Greedy beggars!" he observed, making for the prov-
ender. "Why didn't you invite me, Ratty?"

"This was an impromptu affair," explained the Rat. "By
the way—my friend Mr. Mole."

"Proud, I'm sure," said the Otter, and the two animals
were friends forthwith.

"Such a rumpus everywhere!" continued the Otter. "All
the world seems out on the river to-day. I came up this
backwater to try and get a moment's peace, and then
stumble upon you fellows!—At least—I beg pardon—I don't
exactly mean that, you know."

There was a rustle behind them, proceeding from a hedge wherein last year's leaves still clung thick, and a stripy head, with high shoulders behind it, peered forth on them.

"Come on, old Badger," shouted the Rat.

The Badger trotted forward a pace or two; then grunted, "H'm! Company," and turned his back and disappeared from view.

"That's *just* the sort of fellow he is!" observed the disappointed Rat. "Simply hates Society! Now we shan't see any more of him to-day. Well, tell us *who's* out on the river?"

"Toad's out, for one," replied the Otter. "In his brand-new wager-boat; new togs, new everything!"

The two animals looked at each other and laughed.

"Once, it was nothing but sailing," said the Rat. "Then he tired of that and took to punting. Nothing would please him but to punt all day and every day, and a nice mess he made of it. Last year it was house-boating, and we all had to go and stay with him in his houseboat, and pretend we liked it. He was going to spend the rest of his life in a houseboat. It's all the same whatever he takes up; he gets tired of it, and starts on something fresh."

"Such a good fellow, too," remarked the Otter reflectively: "But not stability—especially in a boat!"

From where they sat they could get a glimpse of the main stream across the island that separated them; and just then a wager-boat flashed into view, the rower—a short,

stout figure—splashing badly and rolling a good deal, but working his hardest. The Rat stood up and hailed him, but Toad—for it was he—shook his head and settled sternly to his work.

"He'll be out of the boat in a minute if he rolls like that," said the Rat, sitting down again.

"Of course he will," chuckled the Otter. "Did I ever tell you that good story about Toad and the lock-keeper? It happened this way. Toad..."

An errant May-fly swerved unsteadily athwart the current in the intoxicated fashion affected by young bloods of May-flies seeing life. A swirl of water and a "cloop!" and the May-fly was visible no more.

Neither was the Otter.

The Mole looked down. The voice was still in his ears, but the turf whereon he had sprawled was clearly vacant. Not an Otter to be seen, as far as the distant horizon.

But again there was a streak of bubbles on the surface of the river.

The Rat hummed a tune, and the Mole recollected that animal-etiquette forbade any sort of comment on the sudden disappearance of one's friends at any moment, for any reason or no reason whatever.

"Well, well," said the Rat, "I suppose we ought to be moving. I wonder which of us had better pack the luncheon-basket?" He did not speak as if he was frightfully eager for the treat.

"O, please let me," said the Mole. So, of course, the Rat let him.

Packing the basket was not quite such pleasant work as unpacking the basket. It never is. But the Mole was bent on enjoying everything, and although just when he had got the basket packed and strapped up tightly he saw a plate staring up at him from the grass, and when the job had been done again the Rat pointed out a fork which anybody ought to have seen, and last of all, behold! the mustard pot, which he had been sitting on without knowing it—still, somehow, the thing got finished at last, without much loss of temper.

The afternoon sun was getting low as the Rat sculled gently homewards in a dreamy mood, murmuring poetry-things over to himself, and not paying much attention to Mole. But the Mole was very full of lunch, and self-satisfaction, and pride, and already quite at home in a boat (so he thought) and was getting a bit restless besides: and presently he said, "Ratty! Please, *I* want to row, now!"

The Rat shook his head with a smile. "Not yet, my young friend," he said—"wait till you've had a few lessons. It's not so easy as it looks."

The Mole was quiet for a minute or two. But he began

to feel more and more jealous of Rat, sculling so strongly and so easily along, and his pride began to whisper that he could do it every bit as well. He jumped up and seized the sculls so suddenly that the Rat, who was gazing out over the water and saying more poetry-things to himself, was taken by surprise and fell backwards off his seat with his legs in the air for the second time, while the triumphant Mole took his place and grabbed the sculls with entire confidence.

"Stop it, you *silly* ass!" cried the Rat, from the bottom of the boat. "You can't do it! You'll have us over!"

The Mole flung his sculls back with a flourish, and made a great dig at the water. He missed the surface altogether, his legs flew up above his head, and he found himself lying on the top of the prostrate Rat. Greatly alarmed, he made a grab at the side of the boat, and the next moment—Sploosh!

Over went the boat, and he found himself struggling in the river.

O my, how cold the water was, and O, how *very* wet it felt. How it sang in his ears as he went down, down, down! How bright and welcome the sun looked as he rose to the surface coughing and spluttering! How black was his despair when he felt himself sinking again! Then a firm paw gripped him by the back of his neck. It was the Rat, and he was evidently laughing—the Mole could *feel* him laughing, right down his arm and through his paw, and so into his—the Mole's—neck.

The Rat got hold of a scull and shoved it under the Mole's arm; then he did the same by the other side of him and, swimming behind, propelled the helpless animal to shore, hauled him out, and set him down on the bank, a squashy, pulpy lump of misery.

When the Rat had rubbed him down a bit, and wrung some of the wet out of him, he said, "Now, then, old fellow! Trot up and down the towing-path as hard as you can, till you're warm and dry again, while I dive for the luncheon-basket."

So the dismal Mole, wet without and ashamed within, trotted about till he was fairly dry, while the Rat plunged into the water again, recovered the boat, righted her and made her fast, fetched his floating property to shore by

degrees, and finally dived successfully for the luncheon-basket and struggled to land with it.

When all was ready for a start once more, the Mole, limp and dejected, took his seat in the stern of the boat; and as they set off, he said in a low voice, broken with emotion, "Ratty, my generous friend! I am very sorry indeed for my foolish and ungrateful conduct. My heart quite fails me when I think how I might have lost that beautiful luncheon-basket. Indeed, I have been a complete ass, and I know it. Will you overlook it this once and forgive me, and let things go on as before?"

"That's all right, bless you!" responded the Rat cheerily. "What's a little wet to a Water Rat? I'm more in the water than out of it most days. Don't you think any more about it; and, look here! I really think you had better come and stop with me for a little time. It's very plain and rough, you know—not like Toad's house at all—but you haven't seen that yet; still, I can make you comfortable. And I'll teach you to row, and to swim, and you'll soon be as handy on the water as any of us."

The Mole was so touched by his kind manner of speaking that he could find no voice to answer him; and he had to brush away a tear or two with the back of his paw. But the Rat kindly looked in another direction, and presently the Mole's spirits revived again, and he was even able to give some straight back-talk to a couple of moorhens who were sniggering to each other about his bedraggled appearance.

When they got home, the Rat made a bright fire in the parlour, and planted the Mole in an arm-chair in front of it, having fetched down a dressing-gown and slippers for him, and told him river stories till supper-time. Very thrilling stories they were, too, to an earth-dwelling animal like Mole. Stories about weirs, and sudden floods, and leaping pike, and steamers that flung hard bottles—at least bottles were certainly flung, and *from* steamers, so presumably *by* them; and about herons, and how particular they were whom they spoke to; and about adventures down drains, and night-fishings with Otter, or excursions far afield with Badger. Supper was a most cheerful meal; but very shortly afterwards a terribly sleepy Mole had to be escorted upstairs by his considerate host, to the best bedroom,